FAIRY POEMS

FAIRY POEMS

edited by Daisy Wallace

illustrated by Trina Schart Hyman

HOLIDAY HOUSE • NEW YORK

GRATEFUL ACKNOWLEDGMENT IS MADE TO THE FOLLOWING:

Atheneum Publishers, Inc. for "Sea Fairies" from *8 AM Shadows* by Patricia Hubbell. Copyright © 1965 by Patricia Hubbell. Reprinted by permission.

Valerie Worth Bahlke for "Fairy Fashion." Copyright © 1980 by Holiday House, Inc.

Curtis Brown, Ltd. for "I'd Love to Be a Fairy's Child" from *Fairies and Fusiliers* by Robert Graves. Copyright 1917 by Robert Graves. Reprinted by permission.

Doubleday & Company, Inc. for "How to Tell Goblins from Elves" from *Goose Grass Rhymes* by Monica Shannon. Copyright 1930 by Doubleday & Company, Inc.; and Doubleday & Company, Inc. and The Society of Authors as the literary representative of the estate of Rose Fyleman for "The Fairies Have Never a Penny to Spend" from *Fairies and Chimneys* by Rose Fyleman. Copyright 1918, 1920 by Doubleday & Company, Inc. Reprinted by permission.

Michael Patrick Hearn for "He Who Would Dream of Fairyland." Copyright © 1980 by Michael Patrick Hearn.

Steven Kroll for "Sleep Song." Copyright © 1980 by Holiday House, Inc.

J.B. Lippincott for "Fairies" from *Eleanor Farjeon's Poems for Children*. Originally published in *Joan's Door* by Eleanor Farjeon. Copyright 1926, 1954 by Eleanor Farjeon. Reprinted by permission.

The Literary Trustees of Walter de la Mare and The Society of Authors as their representative for "Dame Hickory." Reprinted by permission.

Macmillan Publishing Co., Inc. for "The Pointed People" from *Poems* by Rachel Field. Copyright 1924, 1930 by Macmillan Publishing Company, Inc. Reprinted by permission.

Morrell, Peel & Gamlen, solicitors for the estate of J.R.R. Tolkien, for "Goblin Feet" by J.R.R. Tolkien from *Oxford Poetry*. Copyright 1915. Reprinted by permission.

Jack Prelutsky for "She." Copyright © 1980 by Jack Prelutsky.

Library of Congress Cataloging in Publication Data

Main entry under title:

Fairy poems.

SUMMARY: A collection of poems by English and American poets about leprechauns, goblins, and other fairies.

1. Fairy poetry, English. 2. Fairy poetry, American. 3. Children's poetry, English. 4. Children's poetry, American. [1. Fairies—Poetry. 2. American poetry—Collections. 3. English poetry—Collections] I. Wallace, Daisy. II. Hyman, Trina Schart.
PR1195.F34F3   821'.008'0375   79-18763
ISBN 0-8234-0371-8

FOR PRISCILLA MOULTON, WITH LOVE

TSH.

CONTENTS

FAIRIES

Don't go looking for fairies,
   They'll fly away if you do.
You never can see the fairies
   Till they come looking for you.

ELEANOR FARJEON

7

THE FAIRIES

Up the airy mountain,
Down the rushy glen,
We daren't go a-hunting
For fear of little men;
Wee folk, good folk,
Trooping all together;
Green jacket, red cap,
And white owl's feather!

Down along the rocky shore
Some make their home,
They live on crispy pancakes
Of yellow tide-foam;
Some in the reeds
Of the black mountain lake,
With frogs for their watchdogs,
All night awake.

8

By the craggy hillside,
Through the mosses bare,
They have planted thorn trees
For pleasure here and there.
Is any man so daring
As dig them up in spite?
He shall find their sharpest thorns
In his bed at night.

Up the airy mountain,
Down the rushy glen,
We daren't go a-hunting
For fear of little men;
Wee folk, good folk,
Trooping all together;
Green jacket, red cap,
And white owl's feather.

WILLIAM ALLINGHAM

9

FAIRY FASHION

They may take strange
Forms, but never say
They can't be seen—
Only they have a way
Of rearranging things,
Of fitting together
Cold lily-silver
Bodies and dark-netted
Dragonfly wings,

A way of using roses
For faces, dew-
Globes for eyes, and
Spider-silks for hair—
Even their clothing of
Faint moonlight is no
Disguise, but just
The common fashion
All the garden wears.

VALERIE WORTH

THE LIGHTHEARTED FAIRY

Oh, who is so merry, so merry, heigh ho!
As the lighthearted fairy? heigh ho,
    Heigh ho!
     He dances and sings
     To the sound of his wings
With a hey and a heigh and a ho!

Oh, who is so merry, so airy, heigh ho!
As the lightheaded fairy? heigh ho,
    Heigh ho!
     His nectar he sips
     From the primroses' lips
With a hey and a heigh and a ho!

Oh, who is so merry, so merry, heigh ho!
As the lightfooted fairy? heigh ho!
    Heigh ho!
     The night is his noon
     And his sun is the moon,
With a hey and a heigh and a ho!

ANONYMOUS

11

SHE

In the darkest part of the forest's heart,
in the bowels of a stunted tree,
dwells the fairy fair with fiery hair
who bears the name of SHE.

she is rare of face, with an airy grace,
but evil fills her breast,
by day she sleeps, by night she creeps,
and the forest knows no rest.

when the black bats fly through the cold night sky
she leaves her bed of ferns,
and softly moves on cloven hooves,
as the earth beneath her burns.

when the fairy folk, those wisps of smoke
who flit about the flowers,
sit in the shade of a green grass glade,
they whisper of her powers.

they sit and tell of the evil spell
that turned her soul to stone,
and drove their queen of the fairy green
to the deep dark woods alone.

12

now evermore on forest floor
the star-crossed fairy flows,
her fiery eyes slay butterflies
and still the fragrant rose.

do not go near this forest drear
where lives no bird or bee,
beware! beware! of the fairy fair
who bears the name of SHE.

JACK PRELUTSKY

QUEEN MAB

Oh, then, I see Queen Mab hath been with you.
She is the fairies' midwife, and she comes
In shape no bigger than an agate stone
On the forefinger of an alderman,
Drawn with a team of little atomies*
Athwart men's noses as they lie asleep;
Her wagon spokes made of long spinners' legs,
The cover of the wings of grasshoppers,
The traces of the smallest spider's web,
The collars of the moonshine's watery beams,
Her whip of cricket's bone, the lash of film,
Her wagoner a small, grey-coated gnat,
Not half so big as a round little worm
Prick'd from the lazy finger of a maid;
Her chariot is an empty hazelnut
Made by the joiner squirrel or old grub,
Time out o' mind the fairies' coachmakers.

WILLIAM SHAKESPEARE
from *Romeo and Juliet*

*specks of dust

14

PUCK'S SONG

Either I mistake your shape and making quite,
Or else you are that shrewd and knavish sprite
Called Robin Goodfellow. Are not you he
That frights the maidens of the villagery;
Skim milk, and sometimes labor in the quern,*
And bootless make the breathless housewife churn;
And sometimes make the drink to bear no barm;†
Mislead night wanderers, laughing at their harm?
Those that Hobgoblin call you, and sweet Puck,
You do their work, and they shall have good luck.

WILLIAM SHAKESPEARE
from *A Midsummer Night's Dream*

*a mill that grinds grain
†yeast

15

THE LEPRECHAUN

In a shady nook one moonlit night,
    A leprechaun I spied
In scarlet coat and cap of green,
    A cruiskeen* by his side.
'Twas tick, tack, tick, his hammer went,
    Upon a weeny shoe,
And I laughed to think of a purse of gold,
    But the fairy was laughing too.

With tiptoe step and beating heart,
    Quite softly I drew nigh.
There was mischief in his merry face,
    A twinkle in his eye;
He hammered and sang with tiny voice,
    And sipped the mountain dew;
Oh! I laughed to think he was caught at last,
    But the fairy was laughing, too.

As quick as thought I grasped the elf,
    "Your fairy purse," I cried,
"My purse?" said he, " 'tis in her hand,
    That lady by your side."
I turned to look, the elf was off,
    And what was I to do?
Oh! I laughed to think what a fool I'd been,
    And, the fairy was laughing too.

ROBERT DWYER JOYCE

*jug of whisky

17

GOBLIN FEET

I am off down the road
Where the fairy lanterns glowed
And the little pretty flitter-mice are flying:
A slender band of gray
It runs creepily away
And the hedges and the grasses are a-sighing.
The air is full of wings,
And of blundery beetle-things
That warn you with their whirring and their humming.
O! I hear the tiny horns
Of enchanted leprechauns
And the padded feet of many gnomes a-coming!

O! the lights! O! the gleams! O! the little tinkly sounds!
O! the rustle of their noiseless little robes!
O! the echo of their feet—of their happy little feet!
O! their swinging lamps in little starlit globes.

19

I must follow in their train
Down the crooked fairy lane
Where the coney-rabbits long ago have gone,
And where silvery they sing
In a moving moonlit ring
All a-twinkle with the jewels they have on.
They are fading round the turn
Where the glowworms palely burn
And the echo of their padding feet is dying!
O! it's knocking at my heart—
Let me go! O! let me start!
For the little magic hours are all a-flying.

O! the warmth! O! the hum! O! the colors in the dark!
O! the gauzy wings of golden honey-flies!
O! the music of their feet—of their dancing goblin feet!
O! the magic! O! the sorrow when it dies.

J.R.R. TOLKIEN

20

THE FAIRIES HAVE NEVER
A PENNY TO SPEND

The fairies have never a penny to spend,
    They haven't a thing put by;
But theirs is the dower of bird and of flower,
    And theirs are the earth and the sky.

And though you should live in a palace of gold
    Or sleep in a dried-up ditch,
You could never be poor as the fairies are,
    And never as rich.

Since ever and ever the world began
    They have danced like a ribbon of flame,
They have sung their song through the centuries long,
    And yet it is never the same.

And though you be foolish or though you be wise,
    With hair of silver or gold,
You could never be young as the fairies are,
    And never as old.

ROSE FYLEMAN

21

HOW TO TELL GOBLINS
FROM ELVES

The Goblin has a wider mouth
    Than any wondering elf.
The saddest part of this is that
    He brings it on himself.
For hanging in a willow clump
    In baskets made of sheaves,
You may see the baby goblins
    Under coverlets of leaves.

They suck a pink and podgy foot,
    (As human babies do),
And then they suck the other one,
    Until they're sucking two.
And so it is that goblins' mouths
    Keep growing very round.
So you can't mistake a goblin,
    When a goblin you have found.

MONICA SHANNON

I'D LOVE TO BE A FAIRY'S CHILD

Children born of fairy stock
Never need for shirt or frock,
Never want for food or fire,
Always get their heart's desire:
Jingle pockets full of gold,
Marry when they're seven years old.
Every fairy child may keep
Two strong ponies and ten sheep;
All have houses, each his own,
Built of brick or granite stone;
They live on cherries, they run wild—
I'd love to be a Fairy's child.

ROBERT GRAVES

23

THE POINTED PEOPLE

I don't know who they are,
But when it's shadow time
In woods where the trees crowd close,
With bristly branches crossed,
From their secret hiding places
I have seen the Pointed People
Gliding through brush and bracken.
Maybe a peaked cap
Pricking out through the leaves,
Or a tiny pointed ear
Upcocked, all brown and furry,
From ferns and berry brambles,
Or a pointed hoof's sharp print
Deep in the tufted moss,
And once a pointed face
That peered between the cedars,
Blinking bright eyes at me
And shaking with silent laughter.

RACHEL LYMAN FIELD

24

DAME HICKORY

"Dame Hickory, Dame Hickory,
Here's sticks for your fire,
Furze twigs, and oak twigs,
And beech twigs, and brier!"
But when old Dame Hickory came for to see,
She found 'twas the voice of the False Faërie.

"Dame Hickory, Dame Hickory,
Here's meat for your broth,
Goose flesh, and hare's flesh,
And pig's trotters both!"
But when old Dame Hickory came for to see,
She found 'twas the voice of the False Faërie.

"Dame Hickory, Dame Hickory,
Here's a wolf at your door,
His teeth grinning white,
And his tongue wagging sore!"
"Nay!" said Dame Hickory, "ye False Faërie!"
But a wolf 'twas indeed, and famished was he.

"Dame Hickory, Dame Hickory,
Here's buds for your tomb,
Bramble, and lavender,
And rosemary bloom!"
"Whsst!" sighs Dame Hickory, "you False Faërie,
You cry like a wolf, you do, and trouble poor me."

WALTER DE LA MARE

HE WHO WOULD DREAM OF FAIRYLAND

'Twas late on an eve in midsummer,
I fell sleeping on the green;
And when I woke in wonder, I saw
What few mortal men have seen:

Changelings, fays, and sprites, a mighty swarm,
All had taken to the air,
And before them passed their Fairy Queen,
She, the fairest of the fair;

And her mantle was of Queen Anne's lace,
Her skirt was of grass-green silk,
And round her crown lay pearls, one, two, three,
As white as a cowslip's milk;

And then came her ladies, one, two, three,
All radiant by her side.
"Come hither," she cried, "sweet bonny knight!
Take a fairy for your bride!"

And one wore a gown of wild thyme blooms,
One wore bluebells in her hair,
And one bore a cloak of elder leaves,
Each was fairer than the fair.

"Then who shall ye choose, my bonny knight?
Pray, which of my ladies, one, two, three?"
" 'Tis none of thy maidens, lady fair—
'Tis *thee* that I choose, 'tis *thee!*"

"So that's who ye choose, my bonny knight?
Ah, what fools ye mortals be!
Ye're not the first of my suitors, and—
'Tis *I* who must choose, not *ye!*"

Without another word she faded
Like grey mist upon the moor,
And she left me there alone again,
Just as I had been before.

MICHAEL PATRICK HEARN

29

SEA FAIRIES

Look in the caves at the edge of the sea
If you seek the fairies of spray,
They thrive in the dampness of sea and tide,
With conch for breakfast and lobsters to ride,
With gulls to fly and tides to boom
And the long, white, wandering waves to roam.
Look in the caves! Look in the caves!
When spray fairies hide they flee for caves!
They capture a starfish and fling him high
Till he hooks on the edge of the cloud-borne sky
And there he'll dry till they fetch him down,
The mischievous fairies that live in the foam,
The wayward, white-winged fairies of spray
That ride green lobsters out of the bay
Then float back in on a horseshoe crab,
Scamper and turn and dash for their caves,
Swept by the waves.
Look in the caves! Look in the caves!

PATRICIA HUBBELL

SLEEP SONG

How far and wide the fairies fly
On bright and golden wing,
But when they settle down to sleep
A gentle song they sing.

Sweet Queen of Night
Soft silver stars
We're glad you are so near
We seek our beds
We rest our heads
Without a moment's fear.

On thistledown
In hidden nooks
We watch the waning light
The joys of sleep
Upon us creep
We wish you all good night.

STEVEN KROLL

32